I'VE NEVER MET MY
GRANDPA

To Saylor and Weston,
and in loving memory of my dad,
who forever lives on in our hearts

I've Never Met My Grandpa is published by
Kind World Publishing, PO Box 22356, Eagan, MN 55122
www.kindworldpublishing.com

Text copyright © 2022 by Shannon Zigmund
Illustrations copyright © 2022 by Mackinzie Rekers
Cover and book design by Tim Palin Creative

Published in 2022 by Kind World Publishing.

Printed in the United States of America.

ISBN 978-1-63894-014-2 (hardcover)
ISBN 978-1-63894-015-9 (ebook)

Library of Congress Control Number: 2022933947

I'VE NEVER MET MY
GRANDPA

SHANNON
ZIGMUND

MACKINZIE
REKERS

Kind
WOrld
PUBLISHING

Eagan, Minnesota

I've never met my grandpa.

I've heard he is wise.

I've heard he is brave.

But I've never met my grandpa.

I've seen pictures of him.

I've heard stories about him.

But I've never met my grandpa.

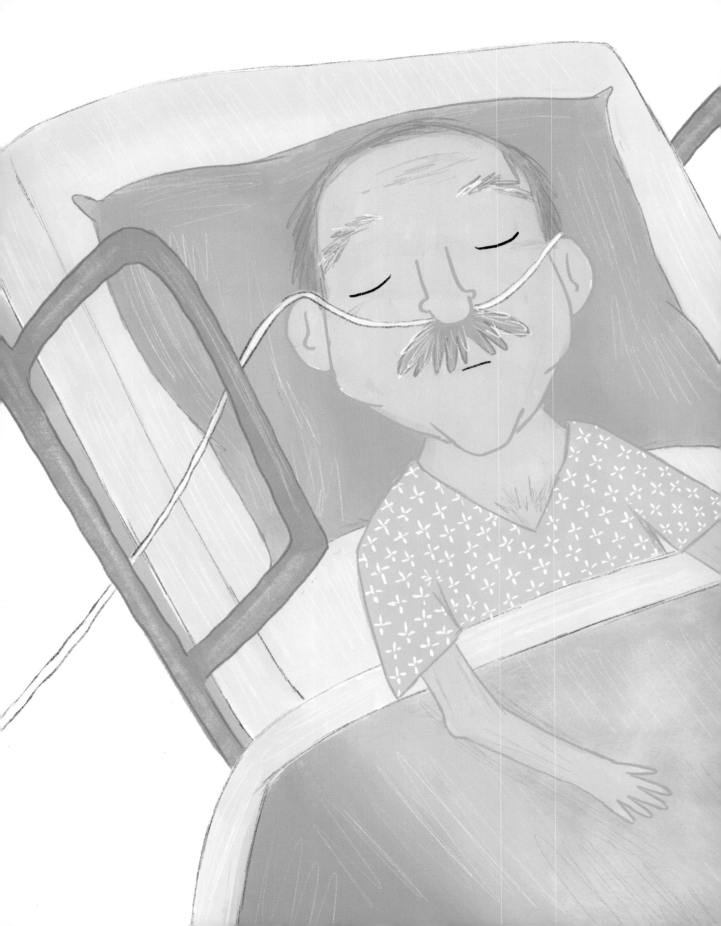

I've heard he got sick before I was born.
I wonder where he is. Can I see him?
I've heard he's in heaven or something like that.
I don't understand.
I've never met my grandpa.

What does he like?
What does he do?
What are his favorites?
Will I like them too?

I've heard he likes jokes.

Daddy tells me a few.

I've heard he likes music.

Mama sings me his favorite songs.

But I've never met my grandpa.

I've heard he plays tennis.

I take some lessons.

I've heard he loves the theater.

I bring Grammy to a play.

THEATER

NOW SHOWING

I've heard he likes parties.

I like them too!

I've heard Grandpa's birthday is coming up soon.

I make him a card using all my favorite colors.

Mama bakes a cake, and we throw confetti around.

I've heard he likes cookies—chocolate chip, just like me.

He likes football and fall and jumping in leaves.

I've heard he likes games,
especially cribbage.

I want him to teach me.

But I've never met my grandpa.

I score the winning goal at my last soccer game.

Mama gives me a high-five like she says Grandpa would do.

I learn how to ride without training wheels.

Daddy says I'm ready for Grandpa's special bike trails.

I've heard Mama crying. She sometimes feels sad.

Daddy tells me it's hard when somebody dies.

Mama says I won't meet Grandpa, not in the regular way.

But she says if I listen, I can feel him everywhere.

I remember all of the things I've heard:
the stories and songs, the games and bike rides,
his bravery and kindness and special high-fives.
And I think, Wait . . . I have met my grandpa.
Mama was right. I can feel him in my heart.

Make a Kinder World

Is there someone in your family who died before you could meet them? What stories have you heard about them?

If you could talk to a family member you never met, what questions would you ask them? What questions do you think they would ask you?

What things does your family do to remember people who have died?

Conversation Starters

The little girl in the story hears a lot of things. Who tells her stories about her grandpa? What does the little girl do to learn more about her grandpa? What questions could the girl ask her parents and Grammy to learn more about her grandpa?